PHOEBE DIGS POLITICS

by Angela Moyle

Illustrations by Ian Coate

Published by VIVID Publishing
P.O. Box 948, Fremantle
Western Australia 6959
www.vividpublishing.com.au

Printed in Australia
Book illustrated by Ian Coate

National Library of Australia Cataloguing-in-Publication data:
Author: Moyle, Angela, author.
Title: Phoebe digs politics / Angela Moyle, author ; Ian Coate, illustrator.
ISBN: 9781925086317 (paperback)
Subjects: Wombats--Juvenile fiction.
Prime ministers--Australia--Juvenile fiction.
Canberra (A.C.T.)--Juvenile fiction.
Other Authors/Contributors: Coate, Ian, illustrator.
Dewey Number: A823.4:

**To contact author or to order more copies of this book,
please visit: www.vividpublishing.com.au/phoebe**

For my hometown, Canberra...

and my amazing family.

If you go to the Land Down Under,
then even a bit further down.
You'll find a wombat named Phoebe,
with a plush fur coat coloured brown.

This nocturnal bare nosed beauty,
really liked her bush burrow hole.
But Phoebe had always wanted,
to get to the green grassy knoll.

For days she waddled her way there,
and finally got to that hill.
The grass was bright green and luscious,
the soil so soft what a thrill!

She started digging her tunnel,
digging deep until she was spent.
She found another odd tunnel,
('twas an air-conditioning vent).

Plodding along this strange tunnel,
she entered a large room of green.
Being her favourite colour,
the best burrow Phoebe had seen.

With wide eyed wonder she entered,
with sure footed waddling steps.
But unbeknownst to poor Phoebe,
she'd entered 'The Great House of Reps'.

Little Phoebe hadn't noticed,
the room contained those making laws.
She padded into the middle,
on her confident stumpy paws.

She froze when someone yelled in shock,
"What kind of backbencher is that?"
With certainty the P.M. said,
"I believe we have a wombat!"

"How'd you get here little fella?
You've caused quite the hullabaloo."
The speaker rang security,
and someone said "Call Ranger Stu."

Phoebe was now rather startled,
how'd she get herself into this pickle?
The nice politicians took turns,
to give her a rub and a tickle.

With all the affection they gave,
it helped her get over her fright.
The room filled up with reporters,
who were thrilled with their scoop that night.

Ranger Stu arrived and said "Phoebs,
this is no place for you to roam."
He placed her in his ranger truck,
and they headed off towards home.

They talked about the Parliament,
and how wombats don't belong there.
It's where they make up all the rules,
and it's not a wombat affair.

RANGER

Phoebe was in the news that night,
it seemed she'd become quite renowned.
"Fame is okay for a while but...
I'm glad to be home safe and sound."

AUSTRALI
NEWS
WOMBAT
VOTE
AU

The glorious end!